Jake's Book

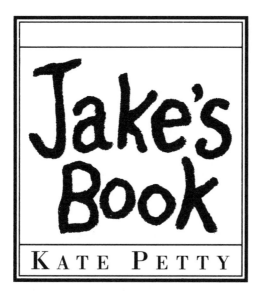

Jake's Book

KATE PETTY

ILLUSTRATIONS BY
SAMI SWEETEN

Julia MacRae Books

LONDON SYDNEY AUCKLAND JOHANNESBURG

Text © 1993 Kate Petty
Illustrations © 1993 Sami Sweeten
All rights reserved
First published in Great Britain 1993 by
Julia MacRae
an imprint of Random House
20 Vauxhall Bridge Road, London SW1V 2SA

Random House Australia (Pty) Ltd
20 Alfred Street, Milsons Point, Sydney, NSW 2061

Random House New Zealand Ltd
PO Box 40-086, Glenfield, Auckland, New Zealand

Random House South Africa (Pty) Ltd
PO Box 337, Bergvlei, 2012, South Africa

Filmset in Century Schoolbook by
SX Composing Ltd, Rayleigh, Essex
Printed and bound in Great Britain by
Butler & Tanner Ltd, Frome and London

British Library Cataloguing in Publication Data
Petty, Kate
Jake's book
I. Title
623.914 [J]

ISBN 1-85681-034-8

Contents

1.	The Skip	1
2.	Little Girl Lost	12
3.	The Bespoke Gent	22
4.	Brothers and Sisters	32
5.	Jake and Dad	42
6.	Angel	57
7.	Jake and the Hamster	70
8.	Lullaby	80
9.	Disappearing Act	92
10.	Christmas	102
11.	Snow	115

1. *The Skip*

Early one Saturday morning Jake
Jenkins heard an extraordinary noise
outside his bedroom window. It was a
scraping, clattering, wheeee-clonk sort
of noise, all at once, and very loud. Jake
pulled back the curtain to see what was
going on.

There, on the other side of the road,
was a huge truck with a crane on it.
Dangling dangerously from the crane

1

was a great metal boxy thing, very scratched and scruffy. Slowly the thing was lowered to the ground. Then two men unhooked it, straightened it up, hopped back into the truck and drove off, leaving the metal box sitting there empty at the side of the road.

Jake scampered downstairs to the kitchen where Dad was making an early-morning cup of tea for Mum. Jake's little sister, Lily, was balanced on one of Dad's feet with her arms wrapped around his leg, making it difficult for him to walk about. "Dad," said Jake, "there's a great big empty metal *thing* in the road. A truck just left it there. Come and see!"

While the kettle was boiling, Jake and his dad, with Lily still attached to one leg, unlocked the front door and peered out into the street. "That's a skip," said Dad.

"A ship! A ship!" shouted Lily.

"A bit like a ship," said Dad, "but it doesn't go in the water. It's like a great big dustbin for people who want to get rid of a lot of rubbish. Usually it's just builders' rubbish – old wood and bricks and plaster. But we'll keep an eye on that skip. I'm always hoping someone will throw out a door I can use in our house. You never know what treasures other people will think are rubbish."

"What happens when it's full up?" asked Jake.

"Well, then the big truck comes back and lifts it up and carries it away to be emptied, and then it can be used by somebody else. Now, how about some breakfast? And Lily, get off my leg!" Lily undid herself and pottered back to the kitchen to talk to Doris the tabby cat. Jake followed and Dad gave them each a bowl of cereal to eat while he took Mum her cup of tea.

When she had finished eating, Lily played quite happily in her highchair, making little trails in the milky puddles and blowing bubbly rasp-berries. Jake found a pencil and doodled on a corner of the newspaper. He drew trucks and dumpers and skips. And when he'd drawn lots of skips, he tried drawing bicycles, though it was quite difficult to get them right. Jake really wanted a bike. But it was a long time till Christmas and even longer till his birthday, so he tried not to want one too hard.

Just as Jake drew two bikes crashing into each other, Lily's cereal bowl hit the floor, *crash*, and Mum and Dad came into the kitchen. But Mum wasn't noticing because she said something that really surprised Jake. "There's a car boot sale at the school today, Jake. Let's see if we can pick up a bike for you there. Perhaps one of the older children will be selling one they've grown out of."

"I want one just like Kaval's," said Jake. "A red one."

"Well, who knows," said Mum. "Perhaps he'll be selling his. We'll go and look anyway. By the time we've finished our breakfast and got Lily ready, it'll be time to go."

Jake went upstairs and pulled on

yesterday's tracksuit bottoms, a clean T-shirt, and two different-coloured socks. He put on his shoes and then he went and sat by the window to watch out for any further developments with the skip.

And there was Kaval who lived on the corner, riding up and down the pavement on his little red bike. Hrrmp, thought Jake. It doesn't look as though Kaval is going to sell that old bike in a hurry, even if it is too small for him. Jake switched on the TV and watched the children's programmes until the rest of the family was ready to go out.

At last. Here was Dad in his jacket and Mum jangling her car keys and Lily all scrubbed and clean with her few sprigs of hair tied in a big bow.

"Ready?" said Mum.

"Ready," said Jake, and off they went.

Jake knew the big school playground well because he walked through it on the way to his school, which had its own special little bit of playground. But today it was full of cars and tables covered with interesting things to sell. Jake and Dad took their time and

looked at everything. Mum had to chase after Lily who had spotted an enormous awful doll that she suddenly wanted very badly indeed. Jake found a whole box full of action figures that a bigger boy wanted to sell for 75p. "But I've only got 50p to spend altogether!" wailed

The Skip

Jake. "Da-ad?"

And it was just as Dad was considering whether or not to let Jake have an extra 25p that Mum came running up with Lily perched on her shoulders. "Quick – over here!" she said. "I've just seen a beautiful blue-and-silver bike for Jake. It looks a bit big and I don't know how much it is, but come and see – ouch!" she finished abruptly, as Lily tugged a handful of hair. "*You* are coming down, young lady, and from now on you are going to *walk!*"

"Carry me?" said Lily pathetically to Dad. So he lifted her up in his arms and they all went over to look at the bicycle.

"Hmmm. It does look a bit big for you," said Dad, though Jake was already in love with the beautiful bike and didn't care what size it was. "Let's ask how much it is."

"Twenty quid," said the man, "and cheap at the price, I'd say."

But Mum was already shaking her head. "I'm sorry," she said, "but we were hoping to find something *much* cheaper than that. Never mind, Jake. Sorry to disappoint you, darling."

And Jake was disappointed. That beautiful bike! Was twenty pounds so very much money? "It is for a bike that's too big anyway," said Dad. "Let's buy those action figures instead." Jake cheered up a bit at this. Mum bought Lily the enormous awful doll, and found a few home-grown herbs in pots for herself. Dad paid a pound for a coffee machine that was old but still worked, so they all went home quite happy and Jake almost managed to forget the blue-and-silver bike.

After lunch Jake made a little set-up with his action figures in the window bay in the front room. He made camps for them under the armchairs and some lay in ambush behind the long curtains. From here he could keep an eye on the skip, too. There were builders in the house opposite and they were filling the skip with all sorts of bits of wood and plaster, just as Dad had said they would.

The Skip

Presently the light began to fade and Mum came in to close the curtains. "Watch out!" cried Jake. "You'll spoil my game!"

"Well, it's time for tea," said Mum, "so you'd better pack up your game anyway." And she started to draw the curtains but paused with them half-closed. "We must tell Dad," she said. "The builders are throwing a really nice door into the skip."

Jake looked outside too. And who should he see but Kaval from the corner riding a *blue-and-silver* bike up and down the pavement! Of all the rotten luck. "It's just not fair," grumbled Jake, and stumped crossly into the kitchen for tea.

Tea was quite a special tea, with jam doughnuts and chocolate biscuits, but it didn't do much to lift Jake's spirits. Seeing Kaval on the blue-and-silver bike had made him feel his disappointment all over again. But after tea he had a very funny splashy bath with Lily and the enormous awful doll and by the time Jake was in his pyjamas and ready for his bedtime story he was in quite a good mood again.

"I want Dad to read to me tonight," said Jake.

"Fine," said Mum, and called down the stairs, "Pa-ul!" The front door was open. Dad was outside grappling with the door the builders had thrown out into the skip. He shouted excitedly from the dark street. "I'm going to need help with this door. But there's something else I've found in the skip that I want Jake to see."

"What is it?" asked Jake from the top of the stairs.

"Go down and see," said Mum, smiling. Jake went down and looked out into the darkness. He saw Dad bent low over something that he was wheeling towards the patch of light by the front door. It was Kaval's old red bike!

"They decided to throw it out," said Dad, "because Kaval bought the blue-and-silver one at the car boot sale. This one's certainly a rusty old thing. The brakes hardly work and it needs a new front tyre – but we know it goes!"

Jake couldn't believe his luck. He wanted to ride the bike straight away, but Dad said, "Absolutely not. You must go to bed now. I'll have a go at fixing the brakes tonight and maybe you can try it out in the morning."

"You were right about the skip, Dad," said Jake as Dad tucked him in. "Kaval thought his old bike was rubbish, but we think it's treasure, don't we?"

2. *Little Girl Lost*

One Tuesday, not long after Easter, Jake and Lily and Mum set off for the shopping centre to buy new swimsuits for the summer.

Everything about the shopping centre pleased Jake. First there was the multi-storey car park. At the entrance was a ticket machine that stuck out its ticket like a tongue when Mum put her money in the slot, and a red-and-white striped barrier that lifted up to let them through. Jake liked driving up and up and round and round as Mum looked for a parking space. Then there were the lifts that carried them down to the shops. Jake and Lily took it in turns to press the coloured buttons. Jake even liked the feeling of leaving his tummy behind as the lift went down, and the shiny sliding doors that opened on to all the brightly-lit shops.

Mum and Jake and Lily headed for the escalator that took them up again, high above a tall fountain that gushed and splashed all day long. Mum folded the pushchair and held Lily's hand tightly as they went up. Jake jumped off the top step and Mum and Lily followed. Just then an announcement came over the loudspeakers: "This is a Lost Child announcement. Would the parents of a little girl called Josephine with long fair hair and wearing a red coat, please come to the information desk where she is waiting for you."

Jake told Mum that he thought it

must be really exciting to have your name read out like that, but Mum said, "Don't even think of it, Jake. Getting lost is really frightening." Then she started to unfold the pushchair for Lily. But Lily had decided to be awkward about everything today and wouldn't sit in the pushchair, so Jake pushed it while Mum held Lily's hand and they found the swimming costume shop.

There were lots of swimsuits to choose from. Mum found four different ones for Lily to try on – a pink frilly one, a tiny bikini, a lime-green one and a red one with balloons all over it. Jake chose three: some trunks and two pairs of shorts in bright colours. Mum ushered the children and their swimsuits into a little fitting-room and drew the curtain across. It was very crowded with all three of them in there. They tried everything on, but they kept getting their elbows in each other's faces and losing their balance as they struggled in and out of their clothes. In the end, Jake chose the red-and-orange shorts, but Lily couldn't make up her mind which one she liked best. So Mum decided for her and bought the one with the balloons.

Then, of course, Lily fussed and fussed because she wished she had the bikini. She cried and whined and wouldn't sit in her pushchair. So Jake very sensibly suggested that they all sat down by the fountain and had a drink and a biscuit, and Mum agreed that that was a very good idea. So they went down the escalator and sat on a bench by the fountain. Mum brought out three boxes of juice and a packet of biscuits from her bag and for a while the three of them were quite content.

As they sat by the fountain, quietly eating and drinking, Mum turned suddenly to Jake and asked, "What's your name?"

"Winnie the Pooh," replied Jake, thinking that Mum had gone completely mad.

"No," said Mum. "I'm serious, Jake. Would you know what to do if *you* got lost? Let's try again. Pretend I'm a kind lady at a cash desk who you've asked for help. What's your name?"

"Jake Jenkins."

"What's your address?" Jake looked blank. "Where do you live?"

"EightyeightAlbertAvenue," said Jake very quickly.

"Well done," said Mum. "And who are you with, Jake Jenkins?"

"My mum and my little sister Lily," replied Jake.

"That's really good," said Mum. "Let's try Lily now, shall we? What's your name, Lily?"

"Lily," said Lily solemnly.

"And your other name?" asked Mum.

"Dane," said Lily.

"All right, Lily-Jane," said Mum. "What's your last name?"

"Denkins," said Lily. She was enjoying this game.

"Well done!" Jake clapped.

"Where do you live, Lily?" asked Mum.

"Home," said Lily, and they all

laughed.

"I'll teach you to say EightyeightAlbertAvenue," said Jake. And he did. All the way home in the car until Lily fell asleep in her car seat.

On Saturday Dad took Jake and Lily to the swimming pool while Mum stayed at home to work.

Dad took the children into the men's changing rooms with him so that he could help them undress. Lily thought the changing rooms with their tiled cubicles and curtains were great fun. In fact she was quite naughty playing peekaboo behind the curtains, but nobody seemed to mind very much. Dad put all their clothes into a locker and blew up their armbands until he had used up all his puff. Then out they went through the footbath and the shower – "Brrrr!" – to the pools.

Dad played with them in the little pool. He gave them piggybacks and pulled them along. Lily squealed and Jake tried very hard to swim. "You're nearly there, Jake," said Dad. "Keep going!" Jake practised going backwards and forwards across the little pool while Dad swam around with Lily on his back.

Then the children were tired, but Dad wanted to swim a few lengths of the big pool on his own. He put Lily in a playpen at the side and told Jake to sit down beside it. Lily was furious. She thought she was far too big to go in a playpen. So she yelled, very loudly, in a voice that echoed all around the swimming pool. Poor Dad had to get out sooner than he wanted, and he felt really quite cross with Lily as they went back into the changing rooms.

He rubbed her down and dressed her as quickly as he could. "Now, for once," he told her, "you are going to sit *quietly* while I help Jake, because he's cold and shivering. Poor old Jake, let's get these wet things off you."

But while Dad was helping to peel Jake's shorts off him Lily crept out of the cubicle and, still quietly, scampered up and down the rows of curtains until she came to the place where you went out. And little Lily went out. She found the stairs that she knew led to the café and climbed all the way up them because she remembered there were nice things in the café. But when she saw all the strange people sitting at the tables, Lily suddenly began to feel very frightened. She looked back at the stairs. Dad was certain to chase after her. He always did. No Dad appeared. A

lot of other people came up the stairs –
and there was a lady in Mum's jacket.
Perhaps it was Mum. "Mum! Mum!"
cried Lily, and followed the jacket between the tables to the other side of the
café. But then the lady turned around.
It wasn't Mum. Her face was all wrong.
Anyway, Mum was at home.

Now Lily couldn't see the stairs any
more. She didn't know any of these
people and she didn't know how to get
back to Dad and Jake. Lily began to
sniffle and then she started to cry in
earnest. Through her tears she saw a
lady in uniform crouching down beside
her. It was the kind lady from the cash
desk.

"Have you lost your mummy?" asked
the lady.

"No," said Lily, and added in a
whisper, "my daddy."

"Ah," said the kind lady. "We'll soon
find him for you. Don't you worry. Let's
go and put a message out over the loud-
speaker. Now, what's your name . . . ?"

Dad and Jake were frantically combing the changing rooms for Lily when they heard the lost child announcement. "Ssh, listen," said Dad, and put his finger to his lips.

"Please would Dad and Dake Denkins of eightyeightAlbertAvenue come to the reception desk where Lily Dane Denkins is waiting for them."

"Little monster!" said Dad, but he was laughing with relief.

"But Dad – she *remembered*! Oh *clever* Lily," cried Jake as they gathered up their things and ran off to fetch her. And of course when Dad picked Lily up in his arms he was so pleased to see her that he forgot to be cross. As for Jake – "Lily, I'm so *proud* of you!" was all he could say.

3. *The Bespoke Gent*

"Wake up, Jake," said Jake's mum.

"Ake up, Dake," said Lily, who was clinging on to Mum's back like a baby monkey. Jake didn't move a muscle. Lily scrambled down from Mum's back. "Ake up, Dake!" she shrieked, and buried her little round head in his chest.

"All right," said Jake sleepily. "Get *off*, Lily – I'm awake now."

"It's Wednesday today," said Mum.

"What happens on a Wednesday?" asked Jake suspiciously.

"Wednesday is Mary Braggins day," said Mum.

"Oh, that's all right then," and Jake snuggled back under his duvet for a few more minutes.

Jake's mum did swaps. This meant that every other Wednesday she looked after Billy Braggins in the morning and picked up Mary Braggins from school with Jake and brought them all home for the afternoon. On in-between Wednesdays, Mary's mum looked after Lily in the morning and took Jake and Mary back to her house after school. That way both mums had a day to get on with some work in peace.

Mary's mum was a dressmaker. She lived on her own with Mary and Billy, and she needed to make a lot of dresses to earn enough money for them all. Jake knew his mum was a 'freelancer', which sounded rather exciting. But all she did was to sit at a desk with piles of boring books and papers – which wasn't really exciting at all as far as Jake could tell.

Usually Jake liked swaps. He especially liked going to Mary's house. Mary and Billy and their mum lived in Albert Close in a tiny terraced house just by the railway. It was more like a cottage than a house – and exactly the right size for children to live in. Jake could always hear where everybody was and what they were doing, whether it was Billy and Lily squabbling in the sandpit in the garden, or his favourite TV programme starting up in the front room. He could hear the 'scrrunch' noise of Mary's mum's scissors and the whirr of her sewing machine as she worked in her bedroom. Mary's cat, Joby, could even hear the sound of the fridge door opening in the kitchen. And though he might not admit it, Jake loved all the beautiful silks and satins and the bridesmaids' dresses that hung on hangers around the house, and the new-shop smell of the rolls of material and the reels of coloured thread and lengths of lace and ribbon. Best of all was the life-sized dressmaker's dummy that stood in the bedroom window. The dummy was often included in their games – as a monster or a wizard – at least, until Mary's mum chased them out of her bedroom, because they weren't supposed to play in there.

This Wednesday when Mary's mum met them from school, Billy and Lily were nowhere to be seen. "Come quickly, you two," she said. "The little ones were asleep, so I've left them. Our nice old neighbour Arthur is there, but he might find it hard to cope with them once they wake up. You know what they're like!"

As soon as they were inside the front door of Mary's house, they could all hear that Billy and Lily were awake. Mary's mum ran straight up to her bedroom and there they were – playing weddings. Lily was struggling into a wonderful long white wedding dress. The dummy was the groom. Billy was going to be the bridesmaid and he had a firm hold on a pale peach creation that was fast slipping off its hanger. They all looked on in horror. And, oh dear, Mary's mum burst into tears. Everyone else went quiet. The little ones stopped their game and looked very guilty indeed. Mary climbed on to a chair and hugged her mum. Jake felt ashamed of his little sister and wished he was somewhere else. And poor Arthur just wrung his hands. He tried to apologise.

"Oh, it's not your fault, Arthur," said Mary's mum, pulling herself together. "Billy and Lily are little terrors. It's just that these dresses have to be ready for a wedding in two weeks. There's another bridesmaid's dress and a pageboy suit that I haven't even begun and there's nothing for lunch and everywhere's such a mess . . ." she trailed off. Mary hugged her tighter.

"Well," said Arthur. "Do you know, Avril (because that was Mary's mum's name), I do believe I'm going to be of some use to you now.

The Bespoke Gent

"First of all, I'm going to take Mary and Jake over the railway bridge to the chip shop and buy some chips for lunch while you deal with the little ones. And then . . . no, I'll tell you my other idea when we've all got some food inside us. Come along, Mary and Jake. We're going on a chip hunt."

Jake and Mary loved going over the railway footbridge. Arthur let them wait and look down while a long train whooshed underneath them before they went on to the chip shop. They looked in all the windows of the little shops in the street too. Arthur smiled fondly at an old-fashioned shop window full of ties and socks and flat hats. He read out the sign above it – "*A. J. Lane. Bespoke Gents' Outfitters.* That used to be my shop, you know," he said. "I had to sell up when I retired. I'm afraid the shop's not what it used to be."

By the time Jake and Mary and Arthur arrived back at Mary's house, Billy and Lily were strapped firmly into highchairs and Mary's mum was her usual self again. "No damage done," she said cheerfully. "The little monkeys were lucky – just a pin missing here and there. And I'm happy to say they *both* got pricked. Now, let's have these chips. I hope you'll stay and eat them with us, Arthur. You've been *such* a help."

"Actually," said Arthur, pulling up a chair, "I think I might be able to help more than you think. You see, I used to work as a –"

The Bespoke Gent

"Arthur's a Bespoke Gent," said Jake. "He showed us his shop."

"He used to sell hats and socks," added Mary.

"– a *tailor*," finished Arthur J. Lane. "I never was much good with the frilly bits, but if it's tailoring a suit for a little lad – well, I can do it in my sleep. Slowly, mind – but I've nothing else to do these days and I'm no good as a child-minder . . ."

Mary's mum opened her mouth but no sound came out. For a dreadful moment, Jake thought she was going to cry again. But she didn't. She walked round the table and hugged Arthur.

"Steady on," said Arthur, smiling.

"Bless you, Arthur. All this time I've been living next door and I've been just too busy to chat to my own neighbour. Fancy not knowing that you were a tailor! A bespoke gentlemen's outfitter, no less!"

After lunch Arthur went home to sort out his sewing things. Jake and Mary begged to come too because they'd never been right inside his house before. Arthur's house was just the same as Mary's, though darker and full of old-fashioned furniture. He even had a tailor's dummy, which he pulled out from under his bed. He found his sharp cutting-out scissors and his pins, his tape measure and his tailor's chalk and laid them all on the big dining-room table (which almost filled the tiny dining room).

"Arthur," said Mary, as she saw all these familiar things, "perhaps you should marry my mum, and then you could always work together."

"I don't think so, my dear," said Arthur with a laugh. "I'm almost old enough to be her grandfather! But nothing would please me more than to run up a few little suits now and then if that would make life easier."

When Jake's mum came to collect her children, Arthur was already hard at work carefully cutting out a pageboy's suit from dove-grey silk. "Well, well,

well," she said to Arthur. "Perhaps you and Avril should set up in business together!"

"Oh no," said Arthur. "I'm too old for business. This is strictly for pleasure. Now, off you run, children – I've got work to do!"

Mary's mum waved goodbye. She seemed to have forgotten how naughty Lily had been – but Jake hadn't. He told Mum about the toddlers' wedding. Mum laughed. "Well, it seems there's no harm done," she said. "Actually it seems to me that something good has come out of Lily being bad, because two people have ended today a bit happier than they started. But –" she looked down at Lily who had fallen asleep in her pushchair "– perhaps we won't tell Lily that."

4. Brothers and Sisters

Jake sometimes wondered what it would be like to be part of a large family. Lily was all right, but there was only her, and she was a girl and couldn't talk properly yet. How would it be to have a big brother, or two big brothers, to tumble about with, and perhaps a big sister as well?

Jake lived next door to a large family. Mr and Mrs Kyriacou had five children

– Androulla, Andreas, Andonis, Leone and Helen. Mrs Kyriacou's sister lived nearby and so did Mr Kyriacou's cousin. They both had children too, and summer days next door seemed to Jake to be one long glorious party. The grown-ups had come to England from Cyprus when they were quite young, so they all spoke Greek together. Jake thought Greece and Cyprus must be lovely places to live in if everybody was like the Kyriacous, and if the smells were as good as the ones that wafted over the fence when the Kyriacous lit their barbecue.

Jake's family always smiled and said hello to the Kyriacous, but because the children were older than Jake and Lily, and the parents were out during the day, they didn't know each other very well.

But one hot day, when all the children were on holiday from school, Jake smelt the wonderful barbecue smell and heard cheerful voices. He took a chair to the fence and peered over.

"Hello, Jake," said Mrs Kyriacou.

Jake didn't know she knew his name. "Hello," he said, feeling shy all of a sudden.

"You want to barbecue with us?" asked Mrs Kyriacou with a smile.

Jake felt even shyer and hopped down from his chair. Mrs Kyriacou laughed. "Another time, maybe," she said, and carried on with what she was doing.

Jake played with Lily in the paddling pool. Then he carried water to the sandpit and made canals. Lily trod all over them and made Jake so cross that he threw sand at her. Lily cried, and that made Mum very cross. "You must never throw sand," she said, comforting Lily and glaring at Jake.

Jake sulked. "Lily's so boring," he said. "She spoils everything. I wish I had a big brother instead of a stupid little sister. Or a big sister, or a *little* brother –"

"That's enough," said Mum. "You go inside and cool off for a bit, Jake. I'm going to stay outside with Lily."

Jake went indoors. He didn't go far.

He sat right by the door, watching Mum watching Lily.

Lily was playing Jake's game. She filled a bucket with water and staggered across to the sandpit, spilling it all the way. She did this again and again, faster and faster, pattering across the grass, which was becoming wetter and muddier with each journey. Jake watched jealously as Lily fetched and carried, fetched and carried, chattering all the time.

Suddenly there was a crash. And then a silence. And then an awful scream, first from Lily and then from Mum. "Oh my goodness!" said Mum. "Oh, goodness! Oh Lily, my precious, are you all right?"

Lily had slipped in the mud and banged her head on the brick edge of the sandpit. Blood was pouring from her forehead.

"Oh dear, what can I do?" wailed Mum as Jake ran out to see what *he* could do. Suddenly he loved Lily more than anyone in the whole world. He cried, "Oh Lily, poor Lily."

And then in the midst of all this commotion a kind and comforting voice came from over the fence. It was Mrs Kyriacou.

"The poor little girl," she said. Then – "Andreas?" she called to her oldest boy, who was nineteen and went out to work. "You must drive Mrs Jenkins and little Lily to the casualty in the hospital. They'll soon have her right. Lots of blood but not too bad, really," she added. "Lily will be fine. And you, Jake, you come and help us barbecue after all. Lily will be home and fine soon."

Andreas was at the front door, jingling his keys. "Pity I don't have a flashing blue light," he joked with Mum. Mum hugged Lily close to her and climbed into Andreas's car. Mrs Kyriacou picked up Jake, even though he was quite heavy these days, and hugged him, and together they waved goodbye.

Jake was tearful but Mrs Kyriacou was kind and consoling. Jake followed her into her house. It seemed much newer inside than his own, full of interesting pictures and ornaments to look at.

Outside, the garden was paved, and there were great tubs of bright flowers. Mrs Kyriacou showed him the barbecue.

"Don't touch," she said. "We don't want you to burn yourself and go to hospital too, do we?"

Jake looked at the smoking pieces of black charcoal. Some of them were beginning to glow red.

In the cool kitchen Androulla, who was nearly grown up, was chopping lettuce and onions for a salad. "Hello, Jake," she said with a smile. "Want to help?" Helen, who was twelve, laughed. "We don't want him to chop his fingers off, though, do we?" Jake didn't think that was quite a laughing matter, with his little sister in hospital at this very moment. Just then Andonis, who was ten and the youngest, passed through.

"Hi Jake," he said. (All these people

who knew Jake's name!) "Want an ice cream?"

"Yes please," said Jake, as Andonis delved into the freezer and handed him one. "Thank you," he added politely.

"I'm Andy, by the way," said Andonis. "Want to play football?"

Jake followed Andy out into the garden. He couldn't believe his luck – playing football with this big boy. It was like having a big brother.

"Goal!" cheered Andy as yet another ball whizzed past Jake – and "Goal!" as the next one went between Jake's legs. "Come on, shorty. Your turn now."

Jake missed his first kick.

He fell over the second.

So then he picked up the ball and tried to run past Andy.

"Foul!" cried Andy. And then, just as Jake was beginning to think a big brother might not be such a good idea after all, Andy whisked him up in the air. "Want a piggyback?" he asked, and swung Jake on to his back. He cantered all round the garden like that. Jake giggled and squealed as he bounced up and down. This was fun!

Andy's cousins started to arrive then. The garden seemed to fill up with small boys. It was also filling up with the delicious smell of barbecuing.

"Hi, Jake!" – all the boys seemed to know Jake's name. They had piggyback races until Tony, one of the cousins, wanted to play football again and suddenly they seemed to forget Jake.

He wandered over to Mrs Kyriacou. "Hello darling," she said. "Having a good time? Want some food?"

"Here, Jake." Helen offered him a plate of food and sat down with him. Leone, who was eleven, came out too and sat on the other side. "Hello, Jake."

Jake ate his food and felt very happy with such kind people around him. Everyone was eating and talking and smiling. He *did* like being at the Kyriacous.

More people kept arriving. Jake looked up to see a tall man who looked just like his dad. It *was* his dad.

"Hello Jake," said Dad (just like everybody else!) and picked him up.

"Where have you come from?" asked Jake.

"I've brought Mum and Lily home from the hospital," said Dad.

"Are they here?"

"No," said Dad, "Lily's fine but tired, so Mum's taken her home for a quiet time."

Then Jake heard, "Dake! Dake!"

There was Lily, on tiptoe on the chair, peeping over the fence. And there was Mum, right behind her, saying, "Lily, be careful, you'll fall!" but smiling as she lifted Lily up to talk to Jake over the fence.

"Lily had ditches," said Lily, pointing at some black thread holding the cut in her forehead together. "Lily was brave."

Jake didn't know whether to laugh or cry – Lily's head looked terrible, but he could see that she was as right as rain!

"Come back, Dake," said Lily.

"All right," said Jake.

And then Lily didn't mind having a rest. Jake wanted a rest too; all those big brothers and sisters were very tiring. Maybe one little sister was quite enough to be going on with.

5. *Jake and Dad*

"Ake up, Dake," said Lily, hurling herself on to Jake's tummy as usual one morning. "Lily's going to ospital."

"Hospital," corrected Jake – and then he said to Mum as she followed Lily into his room, "Why? Why's Lily going to hospital?"

"To have her stitches out," Mum told him. "And it's Wednesday today," she added as she carted Lily out again.

Jake and Dad

Wednesday, thought Jake. Ah good – and he leapt out of bed. A Mary Braggins day. "Am I going to Mary's?" he called to Mum as he went down the corridor to the lavatory.

"That's right," Mum called back from Lily's room. "And a good thing too, because you'd hate sitting around at the hospital."

"I'd like to go to the hospital," said Jake as he went downstairs to the kitchen.

"No you wouldn't," said Dad as Jake came in. "You'd have to wait and wait and you'd be very bored."

"But I'd like to travel there and see the doctors and nurses. I could help look after Lily."

"No," said Dad. "Much better to go to Mary Braggins."

Lily and Mum looked quite smart for going to hospital. Jake looked at them and then at Dad and himself both still in their pyjamas, and then more than anything else he wanted to go on this exciting adventure with Mum and Lily.

"Absolutely not," said Mum. "It's out of the question. Come on, Lily – we don't want to be late for our appointment. You can have your drink and an apple on the train. Goodbye darlings." And Mum and Lily kissed Jake and Dad goodbye and that was that.

"Come on, old thing," said Dad to Jake. "You're lucky not to go to the hospital. You can have a nice ordinary Wednesday – dull, but restful. Just like mine." He helped Jake out of his pyjamas and found him his blue tracksuit.

Jake didn't like the colour of the blue tracksuit much and he didn't like the sound of a 'dull but restful day' much either. He took a long time to get into his tracksuit.

Then Dad couldn't find his socks or his left trainer. Perhaps I won't have to go to school and Mary Braggins after all, thought Jake, and pretended not to know where his left trainer was.

But Dad found Jake's yesterday's socks and discovered the left trainer underneath them. So Jake was ready to go to school. He sat on the stairs feeling cross while Dad dressed. Just then the telephone rang.

"Answer that, could you?" called Dad from the bedroom. Lily loved picking up the phone, but Jake didn't. He went downstairs slowly and picked up the phone in the hall.

"Hello, who is it?" said the phone.

"Hello," said Jake. "Who is it?"

"It's Mary." "It's Jake," said the phone and Jake at the same time.

"Who is it?" called Dad.

"It's for me," said Jake importantly. "What is it, Mary?"

"I've got mumps," said Mary, "so I'm not going to school and my mummy wants to speak to your mummy."

"She'll have to speak to my daddy," said Jake as Dad grabbed the phone from him.

Jake sat on the stairs again and listened to Dad's half of the conversation. It wasn't very interesting at first — "Oh . . . I see . . . Oh dear . . . Really . . .

Uhuh . . ." – but then it got more interesting.

"Well, Martha's taken Lily to hospital, you see. But I'll sort Jake out –
don't you worry about him. All right –
goodbye."

"There's no one to look after you,
Jake, but never mind. I'll work at home
today. Get your anorak on – I'll just
phone them at work before I take you to
school."

"Oh well," muttered Jake. "I suppose
that's that. Lucky old Lily at the hospital, lucky old Mary with mumps – but
I have to go to school as usual."

Dad put the phone down. He looked
worried. "I've got to go into the office for
a meeting," he told Jake. "There's
nothing for it – you'll have to come with
me. I might not be home in time to pick
you up from school."

Jake didn't look worried – a big smile
spread across his face and he hugged
Dad round the knees.

"Come on, then, son," said Dad, "let's
go."

Jake and Dad

Jake and Dad walked to the station because Mum and Lily had taken the car. It was quite a long way and Dad walked faster than Jake. At the station Dad showed them his pass and they went on to the platform. "Don't I get a ticket?" asked Jake.

"No, you're too young to need a ticket." Jake felt rather disappointed.

But then the train came. It was crowded and Jake had to sit on Dad's lap. He felt very small among all these grown-ups going to work – but it had to be far more exciting than going to school.

"When will we get there?" Jake asked.

"Soon," said Dad. Nobody else was talking very much.

At last they arrived at Dad's station. Usually Dad walked to work from here, but he realised that Jake would never keep up with him – so he suddenly did something very wonderful and grand. He stepped into the road, waved his hand and called, "Taxi!"

A taxi! Jake couldn't believe his luck as a big black cab drew up at the kerb right by them. He climbed into the back with Dad.

"Where to?" asked the driver.

"Norrington Gardens," said Dad, still sounding rather grand. "Number 25, just off Argyle Street. I don't do *this* every day!" he added. "But something already tells me that today is going to be anything *but* dull and restful!"

Jake looked out at the busy street – so many people and buses and cars – all rushing to work. He couldn't imagine any of Dad's days being dull and restful.

In no time at all the taxi had pulled up outside 25 Norrington Gardens. Dad and Jake climbed out, and Dad paid the fare. Jake had never been to Dad's work before.

They went into a big hall with a tall desk in the middle. An oldish man said, "Hello, Mr Jenkins" to Dad. He smiled over the top of the desk at Jake. "I see young Master Jenkins has come to the office today as well." Jake felt shy, but he liked the way the man called him Master Jenkins.

Then he and Dad went in a lift up to the fourth floor. People got in and out at each floor. They all smiled at Dad and said, "Hello, Mr Jenkins" and Jake felt shyer than ever, but he was enjoying himself. On the fourth floor they stepped out of the lift. This was Dad's office and everybody said, "Hello, Paul!" and "Hello, Jake! Have you come to help us today?" and "You'll have to work hard today, Jake!" and "Didn't your dad tell you, Jake? We work people hard here . . . "

Jake squeezed Dad's hand. "They're only joking," whispered Dad, and Jake felt better. Jake followed Dad into the room where he worked. The whole room seemed to buzz quietly with telephones and computer screens. It wasn't like anywhere Jake had ever been before. He held very tightly on to Dad.

"Paul?" A pretty and highly scented lady came over to them. "Paul, they're waiting for you in there – all ready to tear you limb from limb, and – oh!" She made the face people make when they coo over babies. "This must be your gorgeous little boy . . ." Jake backed away. "Leave him with me – much more fun than typing letters."

And Dad was gone – into a room to be torn limb from limb, leaving Jake with this brightly coloured, strongly per-fumed girl. Jake's lip trembled. "Actually," he said, "I'm quite big. And I don't want anyone to hurt Dad. I think I'd better go and look after him." Jake tried to follow after Dad, but the lady roared with laughter and caught him. Then she saw his serious face and became quite serious herself. She sat Jake down and talked to him in a very grown-up way.

"It's all right, Jake. We are all friends here. Daddy is going into a meeting where everyone argues a lot. I was only joking, but I can see now that you're a very grown-up sort of person who doesn't like being teased. Neither do I much, so I know how you feel. Now, my name is Sandy and I'm going to look after you while your dad is in his meeting. Let's go and check that he's OK first, shall we?"

"No, it's all right," said Jake, because he had seen a wonderful pot of felt-tipped pens in all the colours of the rainbow and some paper. "What are we going to do?"

Sandy smiled. "Would you like to draw a picture for my noticeboard?" She passed him the pens and some paper. Jake drew a picture of a taxi while Sandy typed a letter.

"That's beautiful," said Sandy. Jake smiled. He liked Sandy now. "Would you like to come and help me do some photocopying?"

"Yes please," said Jake. They found a big square machine with a bright light that flashed on and off. Jake watched as Sandy fed sheets of paper in at one end, and picked up exact copies from the other. "Can I do that?" asked Jake.

"You can do something even more fun," said Sandy, and found him a chair to stand on. "Now – put your hands in here –" She lifted the lid of the photocopier and Jake put his hands flat on the glass. CLICK WHIRR . . . CLICK WHIRR; the

light flashed on and off. "Now – you can look at the copies." Jake took the sheets of paper that the machine had churned out. There were two lovely pictures of his very own hands. Jake couldn't wait to show them to Lily.

"Will Dad be finished now?" he asked.

Jake and Dad

"I'm sure he won't be long," said Sandy. "Shall we be naughty and have a peep at them to see how they're getting on?" Outside the door of the meeting room, she lifted Jake up to have a look. Jake could see his dad looking very cross – and the others all seemed to be shouting at each other.

"What's going on?" he asked Sandy, wide-eyed.

Perhaps they really were going to tear each other limb from limb.

Sandy laughed. "Oh, just shouting. As usual. I'll go and offer them some coffee. That usually calms them down." She opened the door and Jake slipped in behind her.

"I don't give a monkey's what colour we choose," – a man with a moustache was saying, – "let's just all agree on one. Goodness, it's so simple, a child could . . ." He stopped as he saw Jake. He looked at Jake. He looked at Dad. "Aha, a child!" Jake shrank. What was going to happen to him? "Come here, child." Jake looked at Dad and Sandy, but they were both smiling, so he went over to the man with a moustache.

"Jake, isn't it?" said the man. "My name is Charles." He shook Jake's hand. "Tell me, Jake, oh Jake of the blue tracksuit, which of these colours do you like best?" Jake looked at a chart full of coloured squares. One of the colours was exactly the same as his tracksuit. He pointed at it.

"Oh wise one," said Charles. "We will rest by your decision. Cobalt blue it is. Meeting over. Let's go and have lunch."

Dad picked Jake up. "Well done," he said, laughing.

"Brilliant," said Charles. "I can see the boy has taste."

"You chose the colour Charles wanted all along," said Dad.

"What's it for, anyway?" asked Jake.

"Nothing very important," said Dad. "Just the background colour for some writing on a page."

"Is that what you do at your work — choose colours?"

"Oh, we have to choose all sorts of

different things – colours, sizes, shapes, numbers . . ."

"It sounds just like my school to me," said Jake, "but school isn't so frightening!"

Jake was very thirsty and hungry and Dad thought that now his meeting was over he would take him home for lunch. Charles came down in the lift with them. "I'll run you to the station in my car if you like," he offered. So they all stayed in the lift right down to the underground car park where Charles kept his car, and rode to the station in style. It was nearly as exciting as the taxi ride.

Dad bought Jake a drink and a chocolate bar at the station, which took so long that the train nearly left without them. Dad almost threw Jake in the door on to the lady and the little girl who were sitting there.

"Mum! Lily!"

"What are you doing here?" asked Mum.

Dad explained everything to Lily and Mum as the train carried them home. It was lucky Jake and Dad had met up with them because they could all drive home from the station in the car.

When they got home Lily had a rest and Jake wanted one too. "It hasn't been a dull and restful day at all," he told Dad. "And I like the colour of my tracksuit now. Cobalt blue ..." he added and fell asleep.

6. *Angel*

One hot Saturday morning Jake woke up quite late. Sunshine streamed through the gaps in the curtains on to his bed. Jake lay there watching tiny specks of dust dancing in the shafts of light.

What a lot of dust, thought Jake – and then he realised that he could actually hear Mum saying those words right outside his bedroom door. Jake heard the vacuum cleaner whining and clonking against things. In the silence after it was switched off there was a rubbing sound against his door. Lily was muttering, "Got to get the grot off. Got to get the grot off . . ." Jake pictured her scrubbing furiously at something as she spoke. "You *are* being helpful, Lily," said Mum.

Lily? Helpful? Jake leapt out of bed. Why, he was *far* more helpful than Lily! He flung open the door. There, sure enough, was Lily with a cloth in her hand. Mum was about to switch on the vacuum cleaner again, and Dad was on the landing polishing a mirror.

"Morning, lazybones!" said Dad as Jake stumbled out in his pyjamas. "Want to join in the fun?"

"What's happening?" asked Jake. "What's going on?"

"People coming for supper," said Dad, as if that answered Jake's question.

"So we want the place to look nice," Mum explained. "And right now it's awful. I don't know how we're going to get it ready in time," she wailed.

"Who's coming to supper?" asked Jake. "Do I know them?"

"One of Mum's old boyfriends," said Dad, grinning at Jake.

"He's one of *your* friends, too," said Mum crossly. "And he's got a wife. And she's about to have their first baby. And they've never been here before and they live in a lovely house where everything's perfect." Then Mum caught Dad winking at Jake. She laughed. "But I still want the house to look nice."

"I can be very helpful, you know," said Jake.

"Good," said Dad. "Come and have some breakfast and then we'll find something for you to do." Jake and Dad went downstairs together. Then they heard Mum saying to Lily, "No, Lily, there's no need to dust the cat," and a yowl as Mum tripped over Doris, so Dad went back upstairs and brought Lily down.

Jake ate his breakfast. "Well, what can I do to help?"

"You could dress yourself," said Dad.
"That's not very helpful," said Jake.

"It is," said Dad. "Because it means I can get on with something else. And then you could play with Lily for a bit."

"That's not at *all* helpful," said Jake. "That's playing!"

"But it would help me and Mum if Lily wasn't trying to help us. And then later you can come with me to the Pick Your Own. Nothing but the freshest fruit and veg will do for the dinner Mum's cooking tonight."

"All right," said Jake, and went upstairs to put on his red shorts and a white T-shirt. Then he played with Lily out in the garden. They made grass pies and pretended to cook them.

"Lily been helpin," said Lily, busily stirring her mixtures with a stick. She picked a few flowerheads and added them to the pies.

"Lily, you mustn't!" said Jake, and caught her hands in his before she could pick any more.

"Want to help!" screamed Lily.

"You mustn't spoil the flowers!" Jake screamed back.

Lily bit him. Jake smacked her.

"Jake! Lily!" It was Dad.

"I was only trying to help," said Jake.

"I won't be cross," said Dad, putting an arm round each of them. "Now, Lily, you're a tired girl and it's time for your rest. And Jake, it's time for you and me to drive to the Pick Your Own."

They all went indoors. The house was beginning to smell very clean. "Thanks for looking after Lily, Jake. You're an angel," said Mum as a sleepy Lily was carted upstairs.

"Oh, it was nothing," said Jake in a very grown-up way.

"What's a Pick Your Own?" Jake asked as Dad strapped him in.

"It's a farm where they grow fruit and vegetables that people can come and pick for themselves. It's more fun than buying them from a shop."

Soon they drew up in the car park of the farm. There were fields all around with row upon row of plants and bushes. Jake could see people moving up and down the rows far into the distance. Jake and Dad went into a barn where a lady gave them some plastic baskets. "Currants in the far field," she said. "Raspberries just round the corner. Courgettes and peas and beans behind the barn."

"Right," said Dad. "Currants first. Come on, Jake." It seemed a long walk to the currant field. The sun shone down on them. It was very hot. When they found the rows of currant bushes Dad set to work straight away, dropping bunch after bunch of first blackcurrants and then redcurrants into his basket.

"I can't find any," said Jake. "This isn't much fun. It's too hot, and I'm thirsty." He tried eating a juicy redcurrant from Dad's basket, but euuchh – it was sour!

"Veg next," said Dad. Off they went for what seemed like another thousand million miles in the scorching heat.

"I'm *thirsty!*" Jake complained.

"Drink soon," said Dad. "This won't take long."

But it did. First they bent down to pick courgettes. They were prickly. Jake soon gave up. Then they stretched up to pick peas. Jake couldn't reach. He soon gave up on those, too. But then they picked runner beans. Jake was used to picking runner beans with Grandad, and he filled a basket very quickly.

"You're definitely the champion runner-bean picker, Jake," said Dad, comparing their baskets as they trudged all the way down to the raspberry field. Jake's throat was now so dry and dusty he couldn't even answer. Dad looked down at the raspberry canes. "There don't seem to be many of these left. Can you see any lower down, Jake? Jake?"

Well, lower down the raspberry canes there *were* plenty of raspberries. And Jake had seen them. He crammed one delicious raspberry after another into his mouth, and felt the juice stream down his dry throat. *That* was better!

Jake stepped out from the bushes feeling rather guilty. Dad took one look at him. Jake's white T-shirt was covered with raspberry juice. The corners of his mouth were stained a purply-red. In his hand Jake held an empty basket. "I don't know where you found them, Jake," said Dad, "but I think you'd better start putting them in your basket!"

Dad crouched down to Jake's level, which of course was where all the best raspberries were, and together they filled both baskets in no time at all. Then they lugged all the fruit and vegetables they had picked to the barn, where a lady weighed them and told them how much they had to pay. Dad gave the lady an extra 50p. "That's too much," she said. Dad pointed to Jake's sticky face and his T-shirt. The lady smiled. "Don't worry," she said to Dad. "We expect to lose a few that way. I'm sure he's been very helpful."

"Yes, he has," said Dad truthfully. Jake beamed.

Back at home Mum was still busy. "Lunch," she said, pointing towards some cheese sandwiches and yoghurts on the table. She sorted through Dad's and Jake's baskets. "Quite a supper we're going to have with all these! Thank you. But I've still got so much to *do!*"

Jake ate his lunch while Mum and Dad bustled about round him. Lily woke up and had to be fetched downstairs and given lunch. Dad was sent off to do more shopping. Mum looked at Jake and Lily in despair. "I wish you *could* help me, Jake. I could use an extra pair of hands. But I'm afraid you really are too little to help in the kitchen."

"I'm not too little!" protested Jake. "I dressed myself and I played with Lily and I picked things with Dad."

"Did you really pick and not just eat?" asked Mum.

"Yes! I was really helpful!"

"Well, I'm impressed," said Mum. "And I *would* be pleased if you could play with Lily."

"I'd rather make food," said Jake.

"Lily make pies," said Lily.

Mum looked at them both. "Actually," she said. "There is a job you can do for me, a really useful job. Go and sit out in the garden and I'll bring everything out to you."

Mum brought out a basket of peas, a big saucepan and a bowl. She showed Jake how to pop open a pea pod and run his thumb down the row of peas so they dropped into the pan. She put the empty pod into the bowl. "Do you think you can do that, Jake?"

"Course I can," said Jake, and set to work. He soon learned how to pop open the pods in just the right place and ping the peas into the pan. Lily took the pods away one by one to add to her grass pies down the garden and didn't bother him at all. When Mum next came out with drinks for Jake and Lily she couldn't believe how well Jake had done. The pan was full of little bright green peas, and Lily was happily playing down the garden with the pods.

Angel

"Jake, you're an angel!" Mum picked up the pan as Dad came down the garden, back from the shops.

"How are you doing?" he asked.

"Brilliantly, thanks to Jake. He's podded all these peas, *and* kept Lily from under my feet. So now we'll be ready for our visitors. But they won't be here for another three hours! What would you like to do? You choose, Jake."

Jake thought. What was the best

thing to do on a hot afternoon? "I know. Can we take my bike up to the paddling pool in the park and have an ice-cream?"

"I can take you to do all those things," said Dad, without any hesitation. "I think you deserve that for being so help-ful."

Three hours later, when they had come home from the park and Jake and Lily had eaten eggs and fresh peas for sup-per, and had a bath and changed into their pyjamas, and Lily was fast asleep and Jake was still awake in bed, Jake heard the doorbell ring.

He crept to the landing to peep at the visitors. He saw a tall man and a tiny woman with a huge round tummy. They were hugging and kissing Mum and Dad.

"What a lovely house," the lady was saying. "And dinner smells just won-derful. I'm sure I'll never manage to have everything so perfect when we have small children!" She suddenly spotted Jake at the top of the stairs. "Is this little angel one of them?"

"He certainly is," said Mum. But Jake had scampered back to bed. His wings and his halo needed a rest.

7. *Jake and the Hamster*

"Goodbye Jake," said Dad. "Be a good boy. Look after Mum and Lily for me." Dad hugged and kissed everybody goodbye one more time and set off down the road. He turned and waved at the corner and then he was gone.

Dad was going away for a whole week. He was going to fly in a big plane all the way to America. "Wish I could go on an aeroplane," said Jake.

Jake and the Hamster

"Want Daddy back again," said Lily, and began to cry.

"Come on," said Mum. "It's still Monday morning and we've got things to do. Like having breakfast."

Jake didn't really feel like breakfast. He didn't feel like dressing much, or washing or walking to school. He didn't want to say goodbye to Mum at school either. "Cheer up, Jake," said Mrs Susan, the teacher. "It's your turn to feed the hamster this week. Joe, Sam, Mary – take Jake off and make him smile, will you?"

Mum explained that Jake felt a bit sad because Dad had gone away. "He'll be better as soon as I've gone, I'm sure," said Mum.

Jake was very tired after school. But he told Mum all about the hamster. "He's lovely, Mum. All soft, with tiny little hands and feet. He's called Grumpy after a dwarf but he's not a bit grumpy. I wish I had a hamster." Jake didn't want much lunch. He just wanted to flop in front of the television.

Just before bedtime the phone rang. Mum called Jake. "It's Dad!" she said. "He's ringing from America. Come and say hello."

"Hello, Jake," said Dad, sounding rather crackly and far-away. "Everything all right? It's lunchtime here!"

Jake laughed. "Don't be silly, Dad. It's dark!"

"Not here it isn't," said Dad. And then, "Glad to hear you laughing, Jake. Mum said you were a bit down in the dumps. But I'll be home before you know it. And if you're very good I expect I'll bring back a little something for you. Now where's that Lily? Can you put her on for me?"

Jake went to sleep feeling better after Dad's phone call.

When Mum went to wake Jake the next morning, he felt *terrible*.

"Umph – umph?" he grunted. It hurt to grunt.

"Goodness me, Jake," said Mum.

Jake could see that she was trying not to laugh. Lily toddled in. Lily laughed.

"Dake *fat!*" she said, and pointed at his face.

"Jake," said Mum, "you've got *mumps.* I should have realised you weren't well."

"I'm not," said Jake. "My face hurts. A lot. But I *have* to go to school today because of Grumpy. He'll die if I'm not there to feed him."

"You're not going anywhere," said Mum. "Don't fret about Grumpy. The others will look after him. Right now I'm going to look after *you.*" Mum hugged him, but that hurt him too. She made him more comfortable in bed. "Try and go back to sleep for the moment. Lily, come with me."

Fancy me having mumps, thought Jake, almost pleased, and snuggled back down in bed. He could hear Mum and Lily going downstairs. He heard the tap going as Mum made him a cold drink. And then he heard them coming upstairs. Mum gave him a drink with a straw, and a spoonful of medicine.

Later Mum came upstairs again to say she'd phoned school and they had told Jake not to worry. Somebody else would feed Grumpy until he came back. She found Jake some tapes to listen to, but really Jake just wanted to sleep.

The next morning Jake felt quite a bit better when he woke up. Mum came in to see him. "Where's Dad?" asked Jake.

"In America," said Mum.

"Where's Lily?"

"Lily," said Mum "has got mumps."

"Can I see her?" asked Jake. "Has she got a fat face, too?"

Jake climbed out of bed. His legs felt wobbly but he wanted to see Lily. He looked round her bedroom door. "Lily!" he laughed. "Lily, you look just like a hamster!" Lily looked like a cross hamster.

"Hurts," she said, and lay down to sleep.

"What a week to choose, eh?" said Mum. "*Two* of you down with mumps and Dad away. Ah well." And she sighed.

Jake got up at lunchtime and went downstairs to watch television on the sofa. He almost liked being ill. Mary rang to say the hamster was fine. Dad rang. "It's breakfast time here," he said.

"Don't be silly," said Jake. "I've got mumps, Dad, and so's Lily. You'll have to bring home a little something for her, too."

"Keep smiling, sunshine," said Dad, "I want to speak to Mum now."

Soon Jake and Lily got very bored with having mumps. Gradually their lumpy faces went back to normal and sometimes they felt better, but then sometimes they felt worse again. They got bored with their books and their tapes and the TV and their toys and Doris the cat.

"I want to go back to school and look after the hamster," said Jake. "I wish I had a hamster. A hamster wouldn't be boring."

"Well, Dad's coming home tomorrow," said Mum. "That's not boring. *I'm* looking forward to seeing him, anyway."

"I wonder what he'll bring home for us," said Jake. "I know, perhaps he'll bring us a hamster!"

"No," said Mum. "People don't bring hamsters back from America. Perhaps he'll find you a toy or some clothes."

"Wow," said Jake. "Perhaps he'll

bring me a computer."

"No," said Mum. "It'll have to be light enough to carry on an aeroplane."

"I'd like some jeans from America," said Jake. "Do you think Dad might bring us both jeans?"

"He might," said Mum. "Who knows?" And she tucked them both up in their beds.

The next day felt like Christmas Eve. Waiting until tea time for Dad to come home was almost unbearable. Jake and Lily had a rest after lunch, because they were both still a bit mumpy, but neither of them could sleep. They heard Mum answering the phone and then she came upstairs. "That was Dad ringing from the airport," she said. "He'll be home in about an hour."

"An *hour!*" groaned Jake. An *hour* seemed like an *age*.

"So we're going to walk to the shops and buy something nice for tea," finished Mum.

"But what if Dad comes home and

we're out?" asked Jake.

"He won't," said Mum. "Shoes on. Let's get going."

When they got back from the shops Mum and Jake and Lily set the table with plates and a toast rack and biscuits and cakes, a really special tea. "I'll just put the kettle on – that always brings Dad home," said Mum.

And it did. They heard a key turning in the lock and there was Dad. "Hello everybody, I'm home!" he called. "And it's tea time, I see. Well, they're just having elevenses in America."

"Daddydaddydaddy!" Jake and Lily both ran at him.

"What have you brought us?" asked Jake.

"Kids! You horrible lot," said Mum. "Let Dad get his coat off before you start nagging for presents. Whatever next!"

But as they came into the kitchen, Jake saw Dad make a face at Mum and shake his head and pretend to turn his pockets out.

Jake and the Hamster

"Paul!" hissed Mum in a stage whisper. "You never forgot!"

"I did," said Dad. "I'm sorry, kids. Your rotten dad. I was so busy and rushed at the end of the trip, I ran out of time to go shopping for presents. What are you going to do to me?"

Jake's jaw dropped. Dad – not bringing any presents – when they'd had mumps? How *could* he? But then he saw that Dad looked quite unhappy about it and he didn't like that. So he had an idea.

"Never mind, Dad," he said. "You can buy us a hamster instead!"

"Right," said Dad. And after tea, they all went down to the pet shop and chose a beautiful grey and white baby hamster and a big cage for it to live in.

"What shall we call it?" asked Mum.

"Mumpy, of course," said Jake.

8. *Lullaby*

If anybody asked Jake who his best friend was he would say straight away, "Sam." And then he would think a while and say, "No, Joe." And then he would think a while longer and say, "Sam *and* Joe, actually."

Sam and Joe Sutherland, as you might have guessed, were twins. They lived with their mum and dad and their two big sisters, Lucy and Sarah, in a huge ground-floor flat just round the corner from Jake on Consort Crescent. Mrs Sutherland – who Jake's mum called Chris – sometimes walked Jake home from school. If Mum asked Chris in for coffee, Jake took the twins up to play in his bedroom.

Sam and Joe could be terribly naughty at school, and they could be quite naughty at Jake's house, too. They left his toys all over the place and walked on them. Then Jake was glad when they went home and left him in peace. But mostly he liked being with the twins because they were such fun, and funny too.

Sometimes Chris Sutherland took Jake back to Consort Crescent to play. The Sutherlands' flat was one of the most exciting places Jake knew. It seemed to go on for ever, endless doors that opened off corridors, and behind each door a mass of toys or clothes, or sports gear or books or tapes or videos. The Sutherlands seemed to have a lot of everything. Best of all, they had a music room that was filled with a wonderful collection of musical instruments.

The twins' father, Derek, came from Jamaica. He was a musician – and just about Jake's favourite grown-up. He taught music to children, so he understood them very well, and he was quite happy to let them play on the musical instruments as much as they liked. Lucy played the flute and Sarah played the trumpet. Sam liked the drum kit best, but Joe enjoyed picking out little tunes on the keyboard. Jake banged away at anything he could get his hands on. Derek just smiled and said, "Not bad, Jake, not bad at all." And Jake felt really clever and tried harder to bang in time with the others. When Jake's mum arrived to fetch him, Jake usually didn't want to go home.

One Saturday afternoon Jake was having a particularly good time with the Sutherlands. They had played with the guinea pigs, built a Lego castle, and were going to watch a cartoon video when they had finished playing in the music room. Jake's mum arrived just as Jake had learned to hum a tune on the kazoo. Sam was beating a cymbal and Joe was trying to play the same tune on the keyboard. Derek was playing his electric guitar, smiling and saying, "Not bad, Jake, not bad at all."

Jake's mum was really impressed. "Not bad?" she said, laughing. "I think you're all brilliant! I'm sorry, Jake, but it's time to come home now."

"Can't he stay here longer?" asked Sam.

"Let him stay!" pleaded Joe.

"*Please*, Mum," begged Jake. "I don't want to go home. I want to stay here all night."

Just then Chris came in. "You can stay for supper, Jake. You can stay the night too, if you like."

"What do you think, Jake?" asked Jake's mum. Jake was only making a point when he asked to stay the night – he wasn't sure if he really wanted to spend a *whole* night away from Mum and Dad.

"Well . . ."

"Won't you stay the night?" asked Sam.

"Please stay!" pleaded Joe.

"Well . . . all right," said Jake hesitantly.

"Great," said Sam and Joe together, before Jake had a chance to say any more. So Jake gave a wobbly smile and went off to watch the video with his friends, while Mum went home to fetch his pyjamas and his toothbrush and his blanket.

When she came back, Jake was still watching the cartoon, but he kissed her goodnight – that was strange in the afternoon – and heard her whisper, "Ask Chris or Derek to ring us if you want to come home, darling. I won't mind what time of night it is." And then she was gone.

After the cartoons were over, Chris called everyone for supper. It wasn't quite like supper at Jake's house because it was later and noisier and the food was different. Jake had a boiled egg, but it was runnier than Mum's boiled eggs and he couldn't finish it. And he didn't really like the strawberry ice cream – he only liked vanilla – so he couldn't finish that either. Chris was busy and a bit absent-minded. She didn't notice how little Jake ate. Mum always gave Jake a mug of milk, but Chris just gave him squash in a glass like all the others. It made Jake feel rather grown up. "Come on, Jake," said Sam and Joe, pulling him out of his chair. "Bath time!"

Bath time at the Sutherlands was wild. By the time they had finished playing slides and submarines the bathroom was awash. It was brilliant fun. And Chris hardly seemed to mind at all. "Pyjamas!" she barked, as she mopped the floor, and the three boys went along the corridor to Sam and Joe's room.

"Teeth!" called Chris, as she shoved the wet towels into the tumble drier, and then, "Loo!" as she heard the boys coming out of the bathroom. Finally, "Bed!" she shouted from the kitchen, and off they went, just like that.

"Will we get a story?" asked Jake as he sniffed at his blanket for comfort in the little bed they'd made up for him on the floor. Sam and Joe laughed from their bunk beds. "We could ask Lucy to read to us," said Sam from the top bunk.

"LUCY!" bawled Joe from the bottom bunk, right in Jake's ear. Lucy came in. Jake was a bit frightened of Lucy. She was tall and clever and a tease.

"OK, guys. What shall I read? *Dogger?*" Sam and Joe loved *Dogger*, but Jake worried about the toy dog getting lost. He knew how awful he'd feel if he lost his blanket and couldn't have it with him at bedtime. "Night!" said Lucy as soon as she'd finished the story, and left the room, switching off the light as she went.

It was quite dark in the bedroom. Jake had a nightlight at home. He didn't like the dark. "Sam?" he whispered. "Joe?" But Sam and Joe had fallen asleep during the story. There was no answer.

Jake got up and went to the door. He saw Chris at the other end of the corridor. "Chris?" called Jake.

"Aren't you asleep, Jake?" said Chris. "What's the matter?"

"I can't sleep when it's dark," said Jake.

"I'll leave the light on in the corridor, Jake," she said. "Then we can leave the bedroom door open, OK? Night!"

Jake went back to his bed on the floor. It wasn't so dark now. He tossed and turned a bit, and then sniffed his blanket. He listened to the twins breathing in their sleep. Through the open door he heard Lucy and Sarah and the television. He heard people walking past the window in the street. It was funny, sleeping on the ground floor.

He could hear Chris doing houseworky things and Derek washing up. Later he heard the girls going to bed. The TV went quiet. Then Chris went in and switched it on again. Jake didn't like the sounds coming from the TV. He burrowed into his sleeping bag. He heard someone going into the music room.

Jake nearly fell asleep then, but Chris called, "Coffee?" loudly to Derek and a burst of strange music came out of the music room door as she opened it and went away as she closed it again.

Poor Jake. He was tired but wide-awake and more than anything he wanted to be at home in his own bed, with his own nightlight, snuggling down after lots of stories and hugs and goodnights. Suddenly Jake remembered what Mum had said about going home whenever he wanted. He crept down the corridor, trailing his blanket, to find Chris. He couldn't hear the TV any more but he went into the living room and found Chris reading a book. She looked up at Jake. "What's the matter now, Jake?"

"I want to go home," whimpered Jake.

"Oh Jake, it's far too late to bother Mummy and Daddy," said Chris. "You go back to bed and I'm sure you'll be asleep in no time."

"But I can't sleep," said Jake. "If I shut the door it's too dark and if I open it it's too noisy."

Chris sighed. She wanted to get on with her book. She wasn't unkind but she wished Jake would go to sleep. "Try one more time, Jake. It's quieter now. I'll come and see you in a little while.

Off you go."

Jake went out into the corridor. He stopped outside the door to the music room. Derek was playing the piano. "Derek?" called Jake.

Derek opened the door. "Can't you sleep, Jake?" he asked.

Jake clutched at his blanket. "I want to go home," he said.

"I'll take you home in a bit," said Derek. "But first you just curl up on that sofa there while I finish playing." Jake curled up. He liked it in this room. "Any requests, Jake?" asked Derek. He was playing the same tune that Lily's cot mobile played. It made Jake feel sleepy. He didn't know the names of any tunes. "I just like listening," said Jake.

"That's fine, Jake," said Derek. "Listen away," and on he played while Jake lay quietly and listened ... and fell fast asleep on the sofa.

"Not bad, Jake, not bad at all," said Derek softly, and carried Jake to his little bed in the boys' room. He opened the curtain a bit, so the street light shone in, and closed the door.

When Jake woke up in the morning he felt very pleased with himself for spending the *whole* night away from home.

Mum and Lily came to collect him after breakfast. "Did you have a lovely time, Jake?" Mum asked.

"Not bad, Mum," said Jake. "Not bad at all!"

9. *Disappearing Act*

Mumpy the hamster lived in a big cage. There were ladders and a wheel and a long cardboard tube for him to play in. Jake could hear Mumpy playing in his squeaky wheel at night. But hardly anybody saw Mumpy playing in the day, because he spent most of the day asleep! It was rather a disappointment at first. Jake rushed upstairs after school to visit Mumpy – but Mumpy was curled up with his eyes tight shut. Jake wasn't supposed to open Mumpy's cage without Mum or Dad to help him, but that day he unclipped the little door and poked at Mumpy in his nest, to wake him up. And the little hamster was so frightened he bit Jake. Jake hastily shut the door and sucked his bleeding finger. He never tried to wake Mumpy again.

As Mumpy grew bigger, and needed a little less sleep, he became more sociable. When Jake got up in the morning he would find Mumpy clutching at the bars, waiting to be given a sunflower seed. And when Jake went to bed at night, there was Mumpy, sitting up again, looking like Mrs Tiggywinkle, ready to play. Mum and Dad sometimes let Mumpy out for a run in Jake's room. They shut the door to keep out Doris the cat. Mumpy scuttled about, ever so fast, exploring every corner of the room. After a while, Mum or Dad caught him. Then Jake was allowed to hold him before Mumpy went back in his cage.

Jake was used to holding the school hamster, but Mumpy was little and skittery, and sometimes jumped out of his hands. Lily longed to have a hold, but she was so young she was only allowed to stroke the hamster.

One day Jake came home at lunchtime with his friends Joe and Sam. "D'you want to come up and see my hamster?" he asked them - and they followed him noisily up the stairs.

"Ssh!" called out Mum. "Don't wake Lily! She's only just gone off to sleep."

Jake opened his bedroom door. "I can't see a hamster," said Sam, peering into Mumpy's cage.

"That means he's asleep," said Jake.

Joe started to bang on the cage. "Wake up, dozy hamster!" he shouted.

And Sam joined in, "Wakey wakey! Get him out, Jake. We want to hold him."

"No, I mustn't," said Jake. "I'm not allowed to get him out." He looked hard at Mumpy's nest of shredded paper and thought he must be very fast asleep indeed. "Shall we play with something else?"

"Nah," said Sam.

"Let's see what's on TV," said Joe, and the pair of them were off downstairs, leaving Jake to shut the door behind them.

Jake's mum always liked chatting to Chris, Sam and Joe's mum. They could talk for hours. Jake and Sam and Joe watched two and a half children's programmes before Mum said, "Goodness! Is that the time?"

And Chris said, "The boys must be starving! We'd better go home and grab some lunch before they eat each other!"

Then Jake's mum said, "No, don't go. Stay and have baked beans with us." So they did. The boys all had theirs on trays in front of the television and Mum and Chris nattered on without interruption.

After a while the boys shut the sitting room door so that they could get on with a jumping-around-on-sofas sort of game. Mum got up to make Chris a cup of coffee. She stood still for a moment and listened. "Can you hear what I can hear, Chris?"

"I can't hear a thing," said Chris. "Blissful silence!"

"Exactly," said Mum. "I expect the boys are about to start jumping around on the sofa, and – "

"I'll go and stop them," said Chris.

"No, it's not that," said Mum. "It's Lily. She should be awake and yelling by now."

"I'll get her," said Chris, "and then I can have a look at this famous hamster while I'm at it!" Chris went towards the stairs, banging on the sitting room door as she passed, "Oi you boys! Whatever you're doing, you'd better stop before I come down again!" Then, "Lily, Lily," she called in a cooing voice.

Mum made Chris's coffee and poured some milk into it. The house was still strangely quiet. Chris appeared in the doorway.

Disappearing Act

"The hamster's not there," she said.

"Oh, don't worry," said Mum. "He's only asleep. You can never see him when he's buried in his nest."

"But Lily's not there either," Chris carried on. "She's not in her bed. She's not in her room."

"What?" Mum banged down the cup she was holding, spilling coffee on the table. She ran up the stairs. "Lily! Lily?" It was true. Lily wasn't in her room.

"Where can she be?" Mum flew into Jake's room. "Lily! Lily!" She heard a rustling sound. The hamster? No – Chris was right, the hamster wasn't there either. The cage was empty.

Mum tried to calm down. She listened. She heard that noise again. It was a croaky, rustly sound. Hamsters rustled but they didn't croak. The sounds came from under Jake's bed. Mum crouched down. Something scuttled in the dark – it was very dark . . . There was something big under Jake's bed. "Mmmmrrrm?" It was Lily. Asleep

Jake's Book

under Jake's bed.

"Lily!" said Mum.

"WhereamI?" mumbled Lily, all scrunched up. "Where's Mumpy?"

Somehow Mum managed to haul Lily out from under Jake's bed, and a very crumpled and dusty Lily she was too. "Sssh," said Lily as she sat on Mum's lap, rubbing her eyes. "Mumpy's asleep."

"No, he's not," said Mum, as she saw the hamster flashing across the floor and made a grab for him, catching him with her free hand. "Let's put Mumpy back, shall we, Lily?"

Mum carried Lily downstairs. She noticed a little nip on Lily's finger.

"So what's the story?" asked Chris. "What did you do, Lily?"

"Lost Teddy," said Lily.

"So that's why it took you so long to get to sleep," said Mum.

"Found Mumpy!" beamed Lily.

"Go on," said Chris.

"Mumpy bit Lily," said Lily.

"Ah," said Mum. "So you got him out.

Lily, you're dreadful."

"Shut cage door," added Lily.

"Good girl," said Mum, laughing now.

"Then what?" asked Chris. Lily looked up at her from under her long eyelashes.

"Mumpy went under Dake's bed to sleep some more," said Lily. "So Lily did it too."

"I think we're there," said Chris.

Mum squeezed Lily. "All's well that ends well. I'm surprised the boys didn't see you earlier."

"They weren't looking for her," said Chris. "Speaking of boys, I'd better take mine home," she added, and then called "Boys?"

No answer.

Mum and Lily and Chris went and opened the sitting room door. "Boys?"

Nothing. There was no one to be seen. "I don't believe this," said Mum.

Then Lily giggled. "Dake's shoes!" she called, pointing. And there they were, sticking out from under the curtain. The curtain shook.

"Fooled you!" Jake burst out and Sam and Joe popped up from behind the sofa. "We were hiding for ages," said Jake. "Why didn't you come?"

"Because we were looking for Lily," said Mum, and told the boys what had happened.

"She's the best hider of all," said Jake. "Even better than Mumpy. Lily's invented a new game, Mum. It's called Hide-and-Sleep!"

10. *Christmas*

"Christmas gets earlier every year," grumbled Jake's mum as they wheeled the trolley round the supermarket.

"I like Christmas," said Jake.

"Lily likes it," said Lily, who didn't know what they were talking about.

"Can we buy some crackers?" asked Jake.

"I refuse to buy Christmas crackers in October," said Jake's mum, and everyone forgot about Christmas for a bit longer.

Not much longer though. At school, Jake started to learn carols. "Carols – in November!" sniffed Mum, but she did buy some crackers next time they went to the supermarket. Jake sang, "Pull, pull, pull the cracker, Bang!" every day now, and knew all the words. Lily made up carols of her own. Jake couldn't quite understand why everyone got so bored with his carol and laughed at Lily's, but he was beginning to get very excited about Christmas so he didn't notice too much.

At school they were making stained glass windows from black paper and coloured tissue paper, and Jake was going to be a robot in the Nativity play. "A *robot* in a Nativity play!" snorted Mum, but she helped find silver paper and bottle tops for Jake's costume, and didn't really mind what Jake was, so long as he was happy.

Mum and Dad started to write

Christmas cards in the evenings. Dad did his very quickly and Mum did hers very slowly because she wrote so much inside them. She bought some beautiful dark blue card and some gold and silver pens for Jake to draw his own starry Christmas cards. Jake drew diggers on them instead, which weren't very Christmassy, but his cards looked lovely anyhow and he put them in envelopes to give to his friends at school.

A Christmas card addressed to the whole family plopped through the letterbox. It came from their old friends, the Wetheralls, who had moved away from Albert Avenue to a bigger house up the hill. Inside the card was written:

COME TO OUR PARTY
ON CHRISTMAS EVE
7 O'CLOCK ONWARDS
BRING THE CHILDREN

"That's rather late," said Mum when she read the invitation out to Jake, but then she remembered how hard it was

Christmas

to get the children to sleep on Christmas Eve and thought it might be rather a good idea to tire them out at the Wetheralls' Christmas party.

By now, everywhere was Christmassy, especially in the shops and at Jake's school. He had a Christmas party and a Christmas clown who came to visit. They had a Christmas show where Jake sang his carol (and Lily tried to sing hers, but Mum told her to hush), with a Nativity play in which Jake was a toy robot that one of the children gave to the baby Jesus as the best present he could think of.

But still it wasn't Christmas.

The day before Christmas Eve Mum did a last shop at the supermarket. They bought enough food and drink and loo paper to last them through the holiday and enough cat food to last Doris through the holiday too. They even bought Doris a special tin of shrimps for her Christmas dinner. The trolley was so full that Lily had to walk and Jake had to hold her hand and stop her pulling things off shelves. The two of them stood for ages in front of the sweets. Jake saw a wonderful stocking full of all his favourite sweets.

"Do you think Father Christmas might bring me one of those?" he asked Mum.

"You'd better add it to your list," said Mum and then had to dive after Lily who'd found a little packet of chocolate Father Christmases that she wanted right *now*.

At last they got the shopping into the car and drove home. Dad was back early from work and made Mum a cup of tea while Jake and Lily watched TV. Doris the cat seemed very interested in all the tins of cat food and demanded to be fed straight away. "No one seems to be able to wait for anything any more," said Mum, laughing wearily as Dad opened a tin of cat food for Doris.

"That cat's too fat already," she added.

"Cat food, fat food," sang Lily, coming

into the kitchen. "Cat food, fat food, far-away – Amen," she continued, and everyone laughed, even Jake, who liked Lily's carols now, because they were so much funnier than the school ones.

The next day was Christmas Eve. Jake's house was beginning to look really nice, almost as pretty as his classroom at school. There were decorations round the room and strings of Christmas cards everywhere. The tree was lit up with coloured lights and heaped about with a wonderful pile of parcels.

Mum and Dad and Jake and Lily all dressed in their best clothes for the party at the Wetheralls. Lily had black shiny shoes and white tights and Mum tied some tinsel in her little tufts of hair. Mum told the children to hang up their stockings now, because they would be far too sleepy to do it after the party.

The Wetheralls had good parties. There was food and drink in one room and music to dance to in another. There was an en*or*mous Christmas tree all decorated in red and gold with a tiny present for every child at the party.

Mr Wetherall played the piano and William Wetherall played the guitar, so at eight o'clock when everyone had arrived, they all played carols. The Sutherlands had brought their instruments, too. Jake sang his carol and Derek Sutherland sat Lily on his shoulders so she could sing hers. Jake went and found the twins and Mary and Andy and Kaval who were all watching the Snowman video. Lily and Billy curled up on the cushions behind them and fell asleep. Jake couldn't have slept, he was *far* too excited. He was still very excited and in quite a silly mood when Mum and Dad – looking very cheerful with tinsel in their hair – came to carry the children home.

"Snuggle down, Jake," said Mum as she tucked him up in bed. "The sooner you fall asleep, the sooner Father Christmas will come." After what seemed like ages, Jake fell asleep. He could have sworn he heard sleigh bells in the distance as he finally drifted off.

Jake woke up. Everywhere was quiet and dark. Christmas, he thought. It's Christmas. He felt down his bed for the rustly woolly Christmas stocking. It was there! Jake got out of bed and switched on his light. Then he started to unwrap all the little presents that Father Chrismas had packed into his stocking. A little car. A rubber. A pot of bubbles. A tiny jigsaw. And . . . the wonderful stocking full of sweets! How clever of Father Christmas to know! thought Jake. Jake didn't bother with the rest of the stocking. He started to eat the sweets. One after the other. He ate his way right through *all* of them – more sweets than he had eaten all week, all month – probably all *year*. Jake felt very wide awake.

"Mum! Dad!" he called in a sort of shouting whisper. No reply.

He went and prodded Lily. "Lily!"

Jake's Book

Lily was *fast* asleep.

Jake tiptoed into Mum and Dad's room. "Ksnorrrrrr," said Dad. "Go back to bed. At once," said Mum, in a very un-Christmassy way. Jake did as he was told, but it was no good. He was still wide awake.

Jake went down to the kitchen to talk to Doris, but even Doris was sleeping fatly, dreaming of more food, no doubt, and didn't want to wake up. Jake helped himself to a drink of fizzy orange and then crept back up to his room. Oh, *when* would everyone else wake up?

Four hours later, Dad went downstairs to make Mum a cup of tea. He carried Lily over his shoulder. She opened her stocking as they went. She was a very happy little girl this Christmas morning.

Jake was *not* a happy little boy. He had a tummy ache. He had a headache. He felt very cross. He told Lily off for dropping bits of wrapping paper. He tried to pick up Doris, but she scratched him. He sulked in front of the TV.

"Don't be grumpy, Jake," said Dad.

"Not grumpy," snapped Jake.

"Don't be cross, Jake," said Mum, coming downstairs. "Open this present from Aunty Kath." Jake opened the present. It was a magnet. He already had a magnet. "Don't like it," said Jake.

What a day!

It got worse. Jake had had so little sleep and eaten so many sweets that he was perfectly beastly. Grandma and Grandpa came for lunch. Jake made rude noises when Lily sang her carol. So after lunch, which Jake spent under the table pretending to be sick – "Bwahh! Euuchh!" and tickling people's ankles – Mum took him upstairs for a nap, like Lily. Now Mum *never* did that – and not on Christmas day! Jake fussed and cried and kicked, but Mum said, "No. It's bed for you, young man. Maybe when you wake up there will still be enough time for you to enjoy Christmas before it's all over for another year."

Jake fell asleep. He slept for four

hours. When Mum came in to wake him it was quite dark outside.

"Happy Christmas!" Mum said to Jake. He felt much better.

Jake ate tea. Lots of lovely fruit, and honey sandwiches. Then he opened his main present from Mum and Dad – a Lego castle! Jake was so pleased with it. Grandma and Grandpa helped Dad to build it with him. Lily sang her song.

Christmas

"Away in a manger,
There was a fat cat,
And she had a little baby.
Bang Bang Amen!"

Jake laughed with everyone else.

"Doris!" Mum was calling in the kitchen. "Come and eat your Christmas shrimps, Doris! Doris? Where are you, you silly cat?"

Jake remembered that Doris had gone into the cupboard after she'd scratched him in the morning.

"In here, Mum!" Jake jumped up and pulled open the cupboard door – and gasped!

"Mum!" he called. "Mum! Everyone! Look!"

Doris was purring. And not only Doris. Doris, that fat cat, had had *four* kittens.

"Oh," said Mum, hugging Jake. "Fancy having kittens on Christmas day!" She pushed the cupboard door gently shut and gathered Jake up in her arms.

"Well, Jake, I think it's been a perfect Christmas, don't you?"

Jake looked hard at Mum to make sure she wasn't teasing him. She wasn't.

"Perfect," he agreed.

11. *Snow*

Christmas was over. New Year's Eve was over. Even Twelfth Night was over and all the Christmas decorations had been taken down in Jake's house. The Christmas tree had been trailed into the garden and now lay sadly on its side, waiting to be sawn into sweet-smelling firewood.

Jake and Lily had a job to do. They sat at the table with Mum in front of a huge pile of Christmas cards. They were sorting them. One pile for cards with special messages from friends or new addresses or photographs. Another pile for nice pictures to go to Jake's school for the children to cut up. And a third pile which Lily could scribble on to her heart's content. Lily sat there with a fat wax crayon in her hand, ready and willing to scribble on anything that came her way. Mum pored over all the news of her friends and their families and copied addresses into her address book and dates into her diary. Jake looked at all the pictures on the cards in front of him. There were robins and angels and snowflakes. There were churches and carol singers and children building snowmen. There was Jesus in the manger, Mary and Joseph, shepherds trudging through the snow ... "Do you know what was missing from our Christmas?" Jake asked the company at large.

"Mmmmm?" said Mum, who wasn't really listening to him.

"Skibble, skibble, skibble," muttered Lily, scribbling.

"Snow!" said Jake, almost shouting. "'It's meant to be snowy at Christmas time. Why didn't it snow?"

"Mmmmm?" said Mum. "What was that, darling?"

"It never snows in this house," said Jake angrily, but no one seemed very interested in his outburst so he turned back to his pile of cards.

Back at school Jake and his friends cut up the Christmas cards. They stuck them on to a huge sheet of black paper to make a great big snow scene. And outside the sun shone, or it rained or the wind blew – but no snow fell. In fact, January was really quite a warm month and by February Jake's teachers were looking forward to spring. Books about tadpoles and ducklings appeared on the nature table. Jake's mum and Mary's mum even started talking about their summer holidays.

Then, one early evening as the sun

was setting after a clear blue day, it started to feel *cold*. "Cold tonight, isn't it?" was how people greeted Jake and Mum and Lily as they walked home from the corner shop.

"Cold," said Lily, who wouldn't wear her gloves.

"Freezing," shivered Jake, and stamped his feet as he walked.

That night, Dad switched the heating up. "Going to be cold tonight," he said. "Anyone want a hot water bottle?"

The next morning when Jake woke up he leapt out of bed and pulled back the curtains. He looked outside – the grass was all white. "Mum! Dad! It's snowed!" yelled Jake, full of excitement as he hurtled down the stairs.

"Steady there," said Mum, about to climb the stairs with a cup of coffee for Dad. "And anyway, that's not *snow* – that's frost! Jack Frost was at work last night. When you're dressed you can go outside and see what he's done. The garden is quite magical this morning."

But Jake was looking disappointed. "Didn't want Jack Frost," he grumbled. "Want Jack Snow. Can't build a snowman from frost." And he turned round and went back up the stairs to his warm bed.

Later, after breakfast, and as it was Saturday, Jake went into the front room and drew the curtains against the bright wintry sun so that he could watch the cartoons on television. When his programme had finished and he opened the curtains again, the sun was hidden by cloud. Later still, Mum and Jake went to wake Lily from her nap. Jake opened Lily's curtains, and – "It's snowing!" he cried.

And it really was snowing this time. Large grey flakes drifted down from the sky. They started to settle. Lily came and knelt up beside Jake and together they watched as the snowflakes came swirling and twirling down from the sky.

Jake jumped up. "Can I go out in it?" he asked.

"Lily go out too," said Lily.

"I don't see why not," said Mum, and helped them into their coats and boots and gloves and hats.

Jake and Lily raced around the garden trying to catch snowflakes. Jake caught them on his tongue. Mum came out and caught them on her black woolly coat so they could see the beautiful star shapes of the snowflakes before they melted. The snow was coming down, but the world wasn't white yet. "Come in and get warm," said Mum, when her own fingers and toes grew cold. So they went in and had cocoa and crumpets.

"Maybe there'll be enough snow to go sledging in the park tomorrow," said Dad. "I think we've still got an old sledge in the shed. I'll have a look for it later."

And then it grew dark and the curtains were drawn again against the snowy world outside. Jake and Lily went to bed just longing for tomorrow.

Christmas

Sure enough, on Sunday morning, Jake's and Lily's world was transformed. They looked out on to white roofs and white gardens. People walked down the middle of the road, calling cheerfully to their neighbours, who were shovelling snow from the paths. No cars moved. It looked like a Christmas card!

"Can we go sledging now?" asked Jake.

"After breakfast," said Dad.

"Can we go sledging now?" asked Jake, as soon as he had gulped down a piece of toast.

"When you're dressed properly," said Mum.

"*Please* can we go sledging now?" asked Jake as soon as he was dressed – in a *very* weird assortment of clothes.

"When we're all ready," said Dad.

"Please please please can we go sledging now?" asked Jake as Mum helped Lily on with her wellies.

"Yes," said Dad. "Now." And he fetched the sledge from outside the back door. They all looked at it. It wasn't much of a sledge. "Oh," said Jake in a small voice, looking at the little piece of orange plastic. It was starting to crack at the edges. "Will it go?"

"Oh yes," said Dad cheerfully. "It's a terrific one-man sledge . . . "

And then he stopped as he remembered that Jake and Lily were too little to go on a sledge on their own. "Don't worry. We'll all have fun in the snow, you'll see."

And it *was* fun at first, and so different – the whole family tramping up to the park together, Lily sitting like a princess on the little orange sledge as they took it in turns to pull her. Everyone seemed to be making for the park. There was Kaval with a very smart sledge. And Joe and Sam and all their family with *three* sledges. The Kyriacous were just setting out with armfuls of plastic sacks.

"I wish it could be snowy every day," said Jake.

First Mum went down with Lily –

whooooooosh. "Again! Again!" cried Lily as Mum pulled her up the hill again. Then it was Dad and Jake's turn. Dad sat on the sledge and Jake sat in front of him, between his knees.

"Ready?" said Dad.

"Ready," said Jake.

"Give us a push," said Dad to Mum and away they went. Jake held on tight to Dad's knees as they bumped and slid over the snow – so fast!

"Watch out!" shouted Dad. "Ditch ahead . . ." and bump! Suddenly Jake was face down on the snow with Dad laughing beside him. Jake wasn't laughing. "What happened?" he asked.

"We got thrown!" said Dad. "Now we've got to dig out the sledge." A bit of orange plastic sledge poked out from under a heap of snow near Dad's elbow. But – oh dear – it also poked out from under another little heap of snow near Jake's knee.

"It's broken," said Jake. "Our sledge – it's broken –" and he started to cry.

"Oh well," said Dad. "It was fun while

it lasted. Let's go and break the bad news to Mum and Lily."

Lily was already cross and tired of waiting for Dad and Jake to come back. Her feet were cold and so were her hands. "Lily go home," she demanded. "On the sledge." But when she saw the two halves of the sledge, Lily cried too. "I'll carry her home," said Dad to Mum. "You stay with Jake ..."

"You can ride on our sledges," said Sam and Joe, who had come to see the broken sledge.

"And mine," said Kaval, who had come along too.

"Jake can share with us," said the Wetheralls as they puffed up the hill, pulling their heavy wooden sledge behind them.

"Would you like a ride on my sledge?" said Mary Braggins, arriving on the scene with her mum and Billy.

"We'll stay!" said Mum and Jake together.

Jake had the best morning of his life. All his friends seemed to be in the park in the snow that Sunday. Everyone was happy to give him a ride – he even whizzed down the hill in the middle of six Kyriacous on a long plastic sack.

But even the best times in the snow end with cold feet and numb hands and wet clothes. By lunchtime Jake was happy to sit on a sledge with Sam and Joe and be pulled home.

Dad had tried to mend the broken sledge but it was no use. "Never mind," he said. "I don't expect there'll be much more snow this year."

In the afternoon, when Jake had dried out and warmed up again, they went out into the garden to build a snowman. Dad helped Jake to roll balls of snow round the garden until they got big enough to make a body . . . and then a head. They found little stones for eyes and a carrot for a nose. They carved a smily mouth on him and gave him twiggy arms and another row of stones for buttons down his front. Mum found a wonderful chiffon scarf and a party hat left over from Christmas. "What a festive snowman!" she said.

"I wish it could still be Christmas," said Jake. "Christmas and snow go together."

Dad was wrong. There was more snow. The next day was Monday, but it didn't feel like a Monday. There were hardly any cars on the road and no trains were running so Dad couldn't get to work. School was closed because the teachers couldn't get to work.

"We could have gone sledging again," said Dad, "if only we'd still got a sledge. Ah –" he added, bending down to pick up a rather soggy blue letter that came through the letterbox, "the postgirl's managed to get to work." He looked at the letter. "This letter must have been sitting in a snowdrift for some time. It's all wet – and it was posted in December!"

Mum looked at the letter and saw that it was from her brother in Australia – Uncle Tim. "Silly thing," she said fondly. "He never remembers the postcode. This letter must have been to every Albert Avenue in the city – and there must be quite a few of them. But it reached us in the end!" She slit open the letter. "It's a Christmas letter," she said, and read, "We're sitting here in the boiling sun and imagining you in all that cold weather and snow. I couldn't manage to get anything in the post in time for Christmas but here's a cheque so that you can buy the kids a present."

Jake's eyes were wide. "So there is a bit of Christmas left! Now we can buy a sledge to go with the snow!"

Later that morning Mum and Dad and Lily set out on foot to the toyshop. They bought a beautiful wooden sledge that was big enough for all four of them, just like the one Uncle Tim and Mum used to have when they were children. And because there was still a little bit of money left over, Dad bought another little orange plastic one-seater as well. *Two* sledges! "It had better snow every year from now on!" said Mum, as she and Dad pulled Jake and Lily all the way home again.

They went up to the park that afternoon and Mum took Jake and Lily up again the next morning because Dad had to go back to work. School opened on Wednesday. By Thursday the snow was melting and by Friday it had nearly all gone. But Jake would always remember that, just once, Christmas and snow *had* come on the same day.